PRINCESSES wear Trainers

Written by
SAM SQUIERS

Illustrated by
Annabel Cutler

Little
Steps
PUBLISHING

Princess Ellie wore beautiful clothes, sparkling jewels, dazzling tiaras …

and trainers.

The king and queen would beg her to wear her glass slippers.

'How else can I run like an Olympic sprinter?' Ellie would say.

'Or a famous football player? I need trainers to kick the ball so I can go to the World Cup!'

Go ELLie!

Ellie dreamed of playing in front of a roaring crowd as she tied up her laces.

Princess Ellie found it hard to concentrate on practising her scales. She would much rather play cricket!

Her music teacher was not impressed by her batting skills. 'Princess Ellie! That is very **un**-princess-like, and trainers are not appropriate for playing in concerts.'

'But how else am I to run between the wickets?' Ellie asked.

As the castle was preparing for its very important, very fancy Royal Ball, Princess Ellie was preparing to hit a home run in the courtyard outside.

SMASH!

Ellie was just rounding third base when she heard the ball crash through a castle window.

'Ellie!' the queen cried, rushing outside. 'What have you done now?'

'Young lady, this will not do. Princesses don't run around playing baseball ...

... and princesses don't wear trainers!' the king said sternly.

Princess Ellie sighed sadly.
'OK,' she said, as she made
her way upstairs to change.

Princess Ellie came downstairs in her fancy ballgown and glass slippers. She was very uncomfortable.

'Whose idea was it to make shoes out of glass, anyway?' Ellie grumbled.

As Ellie reached the courtyard where the dancing had begun, she heard a terrible commotion.

'DRAGON!
It's a dragon!' cried the guards.

The party guests were rushing inside in a panic.

Suddenly, a gigantic green dragon
swooped down and SNATCHED up
the king and queen, carrying them away.

The guards tried to give chase, but they couldn't move fast enough in their clunky metal armour. 'Who will save the king and queen?' they cried.

'I will!' said Princess Ellie. She took two strides forward ... and tripped, losing one of her slippers. 'But not like this! There's only one thing to do.'

Princess Ellie took down her fancy hairdo and tied her hair back in a ponytail. She changed out of her ballgown and into her football shorts and shirt.

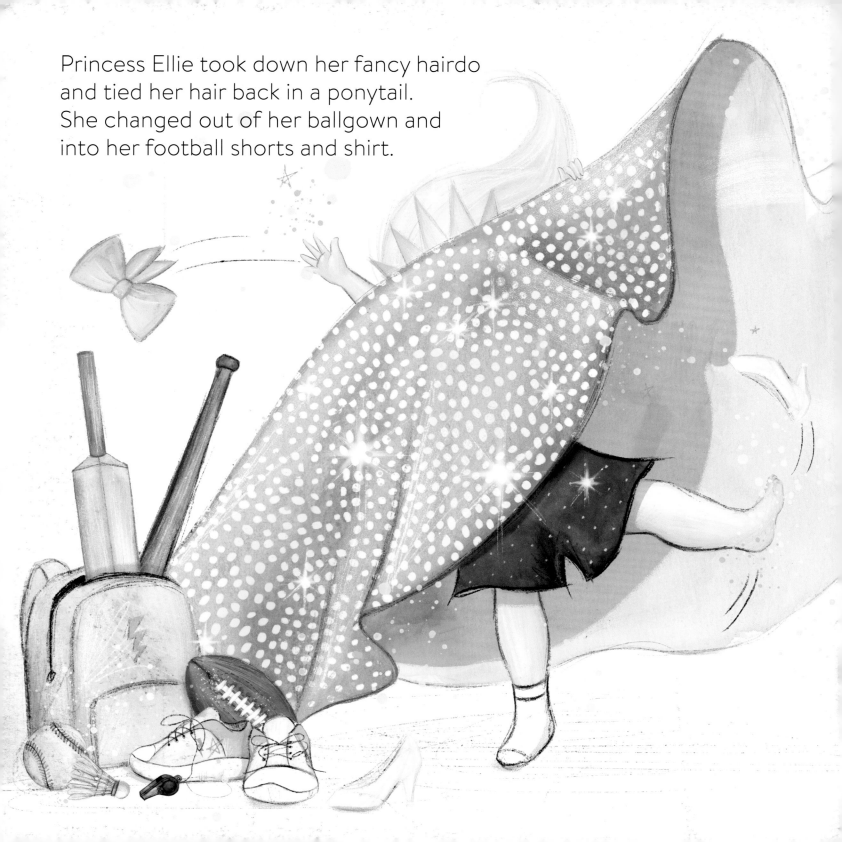

She laced up her trainers and filled up her backpack. She was ready to go!

Princess Ellie chased after the dragon
and ran a whole marathon before
she could see him in the distance.
The king and queen were tied up next to him.

'Hey dragon!' she yelled.
'I can see you. I want my parents back!'

The dragon was tying a napkin around his neck and licking his lips when he turned to the princess's direction.

'Oh, Princess ... I'm quite busy and have a lot on my plate,' he grunted, pointing towards her parents. 'Go away little girl or I'll eat you too.'

Ellie sprinted as fast as she could towards the dragon.
The dragon drew breath and roared out a stream of fire.

ROOOOA

But Princess Ellie stepped to one side,
dodging the flames with some fancy footwork
she had learnt from playing rugby and league.

The dragon tried again.

AARRRR

But Ellie skidded on her stomach, like she was scoring a try and the dragon missed.

The dragon was suddenly out of breath. Only little puffs of smoke came out of his mouth.

PUFF

PUFF

'You'll never make it past this,' the dragon said as he started throwing rocks in Princess Ellie's direction.

'Watch me,' Princess Ellie replied, taking the cricket bat out of her backpack.

HACCCCKKK

CRACK

Ellie hit the rock square on her bat and sent it flying for what would have been a six, but instead hit the dragon right between the eyes.

It knocked the dragon out cold.

The king and queen started cheering, 'Ellie, you were so brave! You defeated that nasty dragon!'

Ellie beamed.

'Things are going to change around here from now on,' the queen said as they all headed back home to the castle.

ROYAL FOOTBALL CUP

And they did.

From then on, the king, queen and every royal subject wore trainers to every occasion.

And the very important, very fancy Royal Ball?

It was now the very important, very fancy Royal Football Cup.

Now everyone in the
kingdom knows ...

princesses definitely
wear trainers.